A Nest of
DINOSAURS

A DOUBLEDAY BOOK FOR YOUNG READERS

A Nest of DINOSAURS

THE STORY OF OVIRAPTOR

Mark A. Norell and Lowell Dingus

A DOUBLEDAY BOOK FOR YOUNG READERS

Published by
Random House, Inc.
1540 Broadway
New York, New York 10036

Library of Congress Cataloging-in-Publication Data
Norell, Mark.
    A nest of dinosaurs: the story of Oviraptor / by Mark A.
    Norell and Lowell Dingus; illustrations by Mick Ellison.
        p. cm.
    Summary: Discusses how the authors became paleontologists and
    describes their expeditions to the Gobi Desert in Mongolia and the
    important fossils they found there.
        ISBN 0-385-32558-4
        1. Oviraptor—Mongolia—Juvenile literature. 2. Fossils—Mongolia.
    [1. Paleontology—Mongolia. 2. Oviraptor. 3. Fossils.]
    I. Dingus, Lowell. II. Ellison, Mick, ill. III. Title.
    QE862.S3N67 1999   98-7859
    567′.912—DC21   CIP
                                                         AC

The text of this book is set in 12.5-point Adobe Garamond.
Book design by Susan Clark Dominguez
Manufactured in the United States of America
November 1999
10 9 8 7 6 5 4 3 2 1

Contents

Introduction
Following the Dream

This is the story of an egg and a nest and something that happened 70 million years ago. It's the story of *Oviraptor* and a nest of dinosaurs, a story we're still trying to understand. It's a story that's changing the way we look at the past.

We are paleontologists, but we study different things. Specifically, Mark Norell spends most of his time studying fossil reptiles. Lowell Dingus studies the 60- to 70-million-year-old fossil-rich rocks that document the end of the Age of Dinosaurs and the beginning of the Age of Mammals.

But besides that, we are professional fossil hunters, and what professional fossil hunters dream of more than anything else is discovering a new place—an untouched spot rich in important fossils that no one has ever collected. For us, that dream came true in 1993 when we discovered Ukhaa Tolgod in the Gobi Desert of Mongolia, in eastern central Asia.

Like most discoveries, this one happened partly by chance and partly through planning and careful execution. Expeditions like the one we made to Mongolia in 1993 are hard to organize. Mongolia is very far away from New York; the weather there can be brutal; and just getting around can be almost impossible, since roads, if they exist at all, are often primitive. First, raising the money for an expedition takes a lot of time and energy. Then, supplies need to be sent months in advance. Finally, finding an experienced crew that can work under extreme conditions and get along is essential. Our Mongolia gang has pretty much stayed together since this first expedition—and we've been lucky enough to make some amazing discoveries along the way.

When our expeditions began, we wanted to look systematically at all the places that might contain fossils in the Nemegt Basin. The basin is a desolate valley in southern Mongolia known for its torrid heat and fierce sandstorms. It's also known as a place where many dinosaurs have been found by Mongolian, Polish, and Russian paleontologists. In this basin lie such famous sites as Altan Ula, Khulsan, Nemegt, and the Tomb of the Dragons. But there are still lots of places to explore, and that's what we intended to do.

One of these places is a small basin inside the larger Nemegt Basin—so small that no one had bothered to look there before, even though scores of paleontologists, including us, had driven within five miles of it many times over the years. This is not a spectacular place; it has none of the large cliffs or extensive badlands that are ideal for fossil collecting. It has only low-lying red patches of earth and a few promontories (jutting high points of land) and amphitheaters (natural "theaters" formed by slopes that surround a flat area). Nevertheless, in July 1993 we pointed our caravan toward the basin and decided to take a look.

As we tried to drive close to the red rocks, our gasoline tanker got stuck in the fine sand that guards the southern approach to the

We cross the desert in caravans along poorly traveled roads, sometimes even following camel tracks.

basin. We were depressed and tired as we took one of the smaller trucks to a patch of red rocks on the western margin. But then we began to find fossils. First came a medium-sized lizard that was rolled up into a ball; then another, identical, lizard; then a dinosaur; and then the skull of a tiny mammal. We named the place First Strike.

We found more fossils, and we wondered: Was this the only spot full of fossils? Or could the entire area be as rich ? It would take us a few days to answer this question, and as it was getting late, we headed back to camp—with our pockets and backpacks full of specimens.

As it turned out, even more amazing things were waiting to be found.

One

Discovering Ukhaa Tolgod

Ukhaa Tolgod today is not a large area; it's only a few square miles of rocky exposures nestled between two large mountain ranges in the southern Gobi Desert of Mongolia. The main fossil-collecting area consists of a series of small hills and low cliffs of brownish red sandstone. (In Mongolian, *Ukhaa Tolgod* means "brown hills.")

Mongolia is a stunningly beautiful country in the middle of the Asian continent. It's sandwiched between Russia and China. Overall, it contains a little more than 600,000 square miles of land. That's about the size of the state of Alaska. It's a big place. But only about two million people live in Mongolia. About a quarter of them live in the capital, Ulaanbaatar.

To get to Mongolia takes us about three days. First we fly from New York to Tokyo, and then it's on to Beijing. Those flights take about twenty-four hours. We usually stay in Beijing for a night and a day before flying on to Ulaanbaatar. That's a fairly short flight, less than three hours. When we've gone from New York to Mongolia, we've traveled about halfway around the world.

From Ulaanbaatar it's about a three-day, 400-mile drive south across the beautiful steppes to our collecting area in the Gobi Desert. When we travel across them in the summer, the steppes are covered with lush grasslands. On the roads we pass magnificent steppe eagles hunting marmots. But the farther south we go, the worse the roads get and the drier the land becomes. There are no

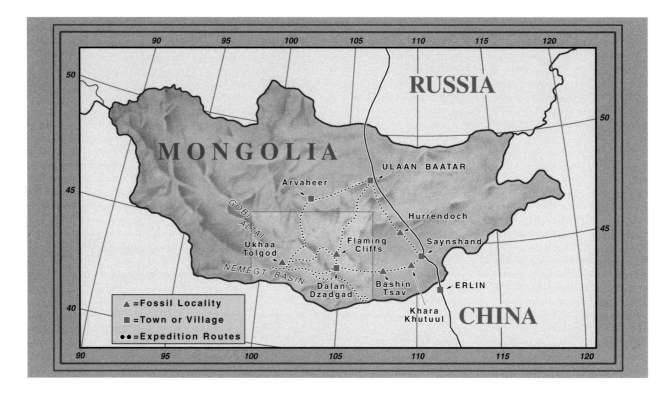

paved highways. The grass disappears and is replaced by small bushes.

To get to Ukhaa Tolgod itself, we must cross a towering mountain range that forms the border of the southern Gobi Desert. The mountain range is called the Gurvan Saichan, which means "Three Beauties." Usually the roads are not so much roads as rugged, gravel-bottomed streambeds that run through the mountains. They are absolutely gorgeous but very treacherous, and our trucks often get stuck in the loose gravel and sand.

Once we've gotten over the mountains, we descend into a desolate desert valley called the Nemegt Basin; that's where Ukhaa Tolgod is. The basin is very dry and rain is scarce, especially during the part of the summer when we're there.

Ukhaa Tolgod is a hauntingly beautiful place of small red hills standing against the flanks of large mountains.

the stars. The night sky is spectacular. Meteors and satellites flash by every few minutes.

Dinosaurs lived at Ukhaa Tolgod about 72 million years ago. The landscape then probably looked much the same as it does today, and by studying the exposed rocks we can get a pretty clear picture of what the area was like. Much of the sandstone in the reddish brown hills represents an area of ancient sand dunes drained by shallow streams.

Occasionally it rained on the dunes. During these rare rainstorms, sand was washed off the dunes and formed small fan-shaped deposits at their bases. Inside the fans root fossils are common, suggesting that water was slightly more plentiful there than on the dunes. Also, most of the fossil skeletons of small mammals, turtles, lizards, and dinosaurs are found in these rocks.

In a few places, layers of ancient mud are scattered among the sand dunes and fans. These probably represent the bottoms of small lakes or ponds that filled during the rainstorms. The lakes probably didn't contain water all year, but sometimes they would have

Daytime temperatures are usually between 80 and 90 degrees but sometimes rise to more than 100 degrees. Occasionally our afternoons are interrupted by violent sandstorms. Fortunately, at night the wind usually dies down and the temperature drops to a comfortable 60 to 70 degrees, so we can sleep out under provided water for the dinosaurs walking through the dunes.

In the sandstone we occasionally find layers of rock that contain ancient gravel. They indicate that there were mountain ranges not too far away. The gravel is too heavy to have been carried by the wind. It was probably washed out of the nearby mountains by streams onto broad alluvial fans like those that form at the mouths of canyons emptying out of the mountains today.

What Was Ukhaa Tolgod Like?

In most parts of the world, the plant-eating dinosaurs outnumbered the meat-eating ones. This holds true for modern animals; today deer and wildebeest far outnumber cougars and lions. At Ukhaa Tolgod, however, this was not the case: Meat-eaters far outnumbered plant-eaters.

Dinosaur plant-eaters are mostly in the group Ornithischia. The word means "bird-hipped." Ornithischians are one of the two large groups of dinosaurs. The other group is Saurischia, which means "lizard-hipped." Saurischian dinosaurs include some plant-eaters (the sauropodomorphs—dinosaurs like *Apatosaurus* and *Diplodocus*) and the

Spectacular specimens like this are usually found once in a lifetime. At Ukhaa Tolgod, we recover similar ones every season.

theropods. The theropods are the meat-eaters. At Ukhaa Tolgod we've found only two kinds of plant-eaters, a small dinosaur distantly related to *Triceratops* called *Protoceratops* and that soaked through the sand or mud, and the shape of the body parts was preserved. It's as if the minerals in the water seeping through the sand and mud filled up molds formed by the original body parts. So, as fossils form, we're sometimes left with a spectacular copy of what the original creature or plant looked like.

The most important job for the paleontologist is to find new fossils and figure out what kinds of plants or animals they came from. In a way being a paleontologist is like being a treasure hunter, combing rocky outcroppings around the world for buried fossil treasures. But being a paleontologist is also like being a detective, searching for clues about what other creatures these plants and animals were related to, how long ago they existed, what their environment was like, and how they lived.

The hills of Ukhaa Tolgod are not dramatic, but they preserve one of our best records of the dinosaurs.

an armored dinosaur called *Pinacosaurus,* a member of the ankylosaur group.

In the Late Cretaceous Period, about 72 million years ago, Ukhaa Tolgod must have been a very scary place. Meat-eaters were everywhere, and there were many different kinds. Besides three kinds of *Oviraptor,* we've found remains of dromaeosaurs (like *Velociraptor*), mononykosaurs (unusual birds), primitive birds, ornithomimids (ostrich dinosaurs), and the adults, nests, and babies of troodontids. All these dinosaurs are fairly small, none more than fifteen feet long. But there were a few big ones lurking around, represented by at least two kinds of rare teeth. These indicate that, while uncommon, meat-eaters as much as twenty-five feet long lived in the area.

The dinosaurs at Ukhaa Tolgod lived during the last period of the Mesozoic Era, the Cretaceous Period. It lasted from 145 million years ago until 65 million years ago. But figuring out exactly how old the fossils are is difficult. One method we use is to compare animals at Ukhaa Tolgod with fossil animals from other places. If they're very similar, we can assume that the fossils from Ukhaa Tolgod are about the same age. For example, some mammals at Ukhaa Tolgod are very similar to ones that lived in North America about 72 million years ago.

But how do we know how old those North American fossils are?

The rocks containing those mammal fossils in North America also contain layers of volcanic ash, and the ash contains small crystals of minerals that were formed when the volcano erupted. These crystals are made up, in part, of atoms that break apart into other

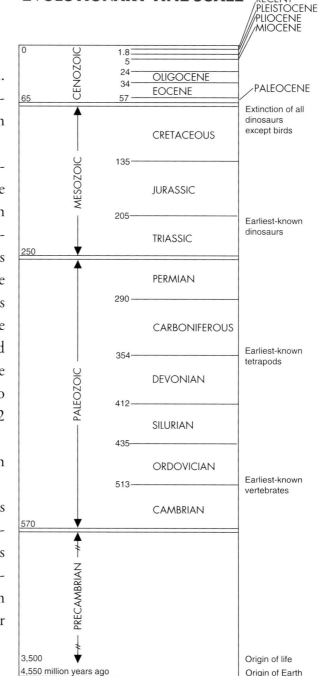

GEOLOGIC AND EVOLUTIONARY TIME SCALE

Era	Period/Epoch	Million years ago	Event
CENOZOIC	RECENT	0	
	PLEISTOCENE	1.8	
	PLIOCENE	5	
	MIOCENE		
	OLIGOCENE	24	
	EOCENE	34	
	PALEOCENE	57	
		65	Extinction of all dinosaurs except birds
MESOZOIC	CRETACEOUS		
	JURASSIC	135	
	TRIASSIC	205	Earliest-known dinosaurs
		250	
PALEOZOIC	PERMIAN		
	CARBONIFEROUS	290	
	DEVONIAN	354	Earliest-known tetrapods
	SILURIAN	412	
	ORDOVICIAN	435	
	CAMBRIAN	513	Earliest-known vertebrates
		570	
PRECAMBRIAN			
		3,500	Origin of life
		4,550 million years ago	Origin of Earth

Because ancient animals and plants lived so long ago, geologists and paleontologists have had to develop a special calendar to illustrate these periods of Earth's history. The calendar is called the geologic time scale. It's divided into four major eras. From longest ago to most recent, they're the Precambrian (4.5 billion to about 600 million years ago), the Paleozoic (600 million to 250 million years ago), the Mesozoic (250 million to 65 million years ago), and the era we live in, the Cenozoic (65 million years ago to the present).

Just as the whole geologic calendar for Earth is divided into four eras, the Mesozoic Era is divided into three periods. The earliest is the Triassic, which lasted from 250 million years ago until about 205 million years ago. The earliest known dinosaurs lived in the Triassic, about 230 million years ago. Next comes the Jurassic Period, which lasted from 205 million years ago to 135 million years ago. This is the period for which the movie **Jurassic Park** is named. The Jurassic saw the development of almost all the largest dinosaurs that ever lived. These were the sauropods, a group of enormous plant-eaters such as **Apatosaurus** (formerly called **Brontosaurus**), **Diplodocus**, and **Brachiosaurus**.

It's very hard for people to understand how long ago the animals preserved as fossils at Ukhaa Tolgod lived. Say you're 10 years old. The normal life span for a person living in the United States today is about 70 years. The United States itself is slightly more than 200 years old. The earliest human civilizations based on agriculture that we know about existed around 7,000 years ago. The end of the ice ages, when animals like saber-toothed cats, mammoths, and mastodons became extinct, happened about 12,000 years ago. The earliest members of our human species lived around 100,000 years ago, and our earliest human relatives first walked the earth about 4.5 million years ago. Most dinosaurs died out 65 million years ago. But the animals living at Ukhaa Tolgod lived even before that, somewhere between 70 and 80 million years ago. To us, that's a very long time ago.

atoms at a constant rate. The atoms that break apart are called parent atoms, and the atoms that the parent atoms break apart into are called daughter atoms. The breaking-apart process is called radioactive decay.

Using special instruments, we can measure how long it takes for half of the parent atoms to break up into their daughter atoms. We can also measure how many parent and daughter atoms are present in the small crystals that were formed when the volcano erupted. Once we know these amounts, we can calculate the age of the layer of volcanic ash and find out approximately how old the fossils in the nearby rock layers are.

What Happened at Ukhaa Tolgod?

Another mystery continues to puzzle us, and it's even harder to solve: How did these animals die? Many of the fossil skeletons we've found at Ukhaa Tolgod are nearly intact. It's very rare to discover such complete fossil skeletons, and it indicates that the carcasses were buried quickly after death, before other scavenging animals could tear up the bodies. Some ideas about the way the animals at Ukhaa Tolgod died have been suggested, but scientists still don't know for certain.

One possible explanation is that the fossil animals were killed by giant sandstorms—the kind that engulf caravans in the world's great deserts, like the Takla Makan and the Sahara. Sandstorms can last for several days. We've encountered smaller sandstorms on our expeditions to the Gobi Desert, and they're no fun. The sky turns grayish brown on the horizon, and within minutes you're engulfed in a curtain of sand blowing into your face at fifty or sixty miles an hour. Getting caught in one of these storms feels like getting sandblasted. All you can do is crawl inside your tent or truck and wait out the storm. If you're caught outside, you huddle against the rocks and turn away from the wind, but the sand still gets in your eyes, nose, mouth, ears, and clothing. Several inches of blown sand can build up around your feet or your tents in just an hour.

The Gobi is known for its brutal sandstorms, which can destroy tents and "sandblast" paleontologists. However, these storms often produce spectacular effects that make the discomfort worthwhile.

Still, there are few reports of modern animals actually being buried during such sandstorms. The sand is loose and easy to scrape away from your body. It doesn't seem likely that an animal would just sit there and allow itself to be buried.

That seems to fit with the fact that we find hardly any fossils in the tilted sand layers that formed the actively migrating sand dunes.

Maybe if an animal was weakened by illness or was injured it could be buried in a sandstorm.

Another possible explanation for the death of these animals is dehydration. Remember, this is one of the world's largest deserts, and water today is scarce. The region can go for weeks or even months without rain. Today, on average, less than four inches of rain falls in this part of the Gobi every year.

Conditions when dinosaurs lived in the ancient desert may have been similar. Obviously, animals like camels are specially adapted to survive such conditions, but many die during extended droughts. Maybe dinosaurs suffered the same fate. Plants on the desolate dunes and sand fans might have died during the long periods without rain; that would have killed the mammals, lizards, and dinosaurs too, since they needed the plants as well as water. If many of these plant-eaters died, the carnivorous predators might have suffered in turn.

However, the reason for the animals' death is still a mystery.

Two

We Find Oviraptor

We weren't the first team to go to the Gobi Desert looking for fossils. We weren't even the first team from the American Museum of Natural History. In fact, dinosaur fossils were first found in Mongolia in the 1920s during expeditions led by a man named Roy Chapman Andrews. Andrews, a legendary explorer of the time, started working at the American Museum of Natural History as an assistant in the taxidermy department—often sweeping floors, for a salary of ten dollars a week. When he left the museum forty years later, he was its director.

The largest of Andrews's expeditions was the Third Asiatic Expedition, an ambitious undertaking whose goal was to find fossils of early humans in Asia. The group didn't find remains of early man, but they made enough other discoveries to put Mongolia on the map as one of the world's hot spots for dinosaur paleontologists.

In the late summer of 1922, Andrews made what would become his greatest discovery. On the afternoon of September 1, the caravan was heading toward Beijing, crossing the great plains just north of the Gurvan Saichan mountains. Andrews stopped near a small encampment of Mongols to ask directions. While he was asking, the expedition photographer, J. B. Shackleford, and the chief paleontologist, Walter Granger, checked out some red rocks in the other direction. As they

Led by Roy Chapman Andrews in the 1920s, the Central Asiatic Expeditions captured great fossil treasures of the Gobi Desert for the American Museum of Natural History.

got close, they realized that this small patch of red rocks was just the top of a large cliff face. Almost immediately they found fossils. But because it was so late in the season, they needed to press on toward Beijing, spending only a single day at the site.

The site, which extended for several miles, was called the Flaming Cliffs because of the orange-red color the bright red hills took on in the evening sun. During the following years, the expedition concentrated on the rich fossil beds of the Flaming Cliffs, making several important discoveries. Among these were the dinosaur specimens that formed the basis of our own work—including the type, or first known specimen, of *Velociraptor, Oviraptor, Protoceratops,* and *Saurornithoides*. Andrews's group also collected specimens of fossil mammals that lived during the time of the dinosaurs. Most importantly, it was in this desolate part of Mongolia that, in 1923, the first nests of dinosaurs were found.

Things have changed since Roy Chapman Andrews rose from floor sweeper to head of the American Museum of Natural History. Now to become a paleontologist you must have a Ph.D. But for us it is worth it.

We wanted to become paleontologists because we both loved being outdoors. Fortunately for us, we grew up in southern California, where there were great places to explore less than a two-hour drive from home. Our outings made us curious about the plants and animals living there, as well as the rocks that formed the landscapes.

The underside of more than one family car was pretty well demolished after we'd bounced over dirt roads in the desert, but these weekend expeditions were what we lived for, and they inspired us to ask the kinds of questions we're still asking today: How did this desert get here? What was it like millions of years ago? What kinds of animals lived here? How did the animals get here?

Over the summer family vacations took us to national parks and national monuments, many of which have visitors' centers where rangers give daily lectures and lead hikes around the parks to teach visitors about how an area was formed, as well as what kinds of animals and plants lived there. Other national parks were also high on our list of places to visit because they explain how geologic forces, operating over thousands and even million of years, create the landscapes of our natural world.

In high school and later, as undergraduates in college, we both volunteered in the Vertebrate Paleontology Department at the Los Angeles County Museum of Natural History. That's where we first met, in the early 1970s. While we were volunteering at the museum, technicians called preparators taught us how to prepare fossils—how to clean the sand and mud off the delicate fossil bones after they'd been collected in the field. The curators and collection managers also taught us how to curate fossils. This involved learning how to identify and store the fossils in the collection. Occasionally we were even invited to go on collecting trips, which gave us our first taste of real scientific fieldwork.

Our curiosity eventually guided our schoolwork. To become a paleontologist, you need a broad education. Of course, it's important to take classes like math, chemistry, biology, and earth science. Learning to write well and to type is an essential tool for composing scientific reports and articles. Some skill in drawing and photography comes in handy for documenting layers of rock and fossils in the field. But it's also important to branch out into areas like foreign language so that you can read papers written by scientists in other countries and talk to them when you go to collect in far-off lands. Even auto repair and carpentry are useful. It's no fun being stuck in the field with a broken truck when you know that spectacular fossils are waiting to be found just a day's drive away.

In college students of paleontology usually pick one of two routes—geology or biology. Both are critical to understanding fossils. If you emphasize biology, you focus primarily on a fossil animal's evolutionary relationships or the way the animal's body works. If you emphasize geology, you study how old the fossil animal is or what kind of environment the animal lived in.

As we went through school, Mark emphasized biology and Lowell focused on geology, so our jobs are rather different, but we both love what we do.

There are lots of great national parks, monuments, and other places to explore. With our families we've visited many of them, such as Capital Reef in Utah.

As soon as the 1923 expedition got to the Flaming Cliffs, the crew began finding dinosaur fossils. White limb bones, vertebrae, and skulls seemed to litter the ground at the base of the cliffs. Fossils of *Protoceratops* were the most common, but there were many types. Before long the team began to find dinosaur eggs, and finally, at lunch on July 13, expedition technician George Olsen announced that he had found what he thought was a dinosaur nest. Immediately the expedition members took off to look at the discovery.

Lying before them, sticking out from the side of the cliff, were large eggs arranged in a circle, just as they had been laid about 70 million years before. At first not everyone agreed that these were dinosaur eggs. Some argued that they were turtle eggs or even the eggs of a giant ground bird. But after all the possible arguments had been tried out and discarded, the scientists were left with the realization that

The first nests of dinosaurs were found at the Flaming Cliffs in 1923.

there, in a remote part of Mongolia, they had found the first dinosaur nest.

Soon other nests were located, and the job of excavating them began. As crew members were digging around the first nest, they got a surprise. Lying on top of the nest were the bones of a small dinosaur. Although the specimen was fragmentary, the large claws showed that it was a meat-eater—a theropod. But what did the theropod dinosaur have to do with the nest of eggs?

Digging Up Dinosaurs

One of the first questions people ask us when they find out we're paleontologists who go on expeditions is "How do you know where to dig?" Finding the right spot takes hard work and a lot of luck. The remains of vertebrate fossils are extremely rare, and you wouldn't be a very successful paleontologist if you just got out of the truck and said, "Hey, that looks like a good place, let's start digging."

Before we ever go on an expedition, a lot of preparation is required. There are the obvious steps, like getting our camping gear together and arranging for food and airline tickets. More importantly, we have to study all the relevant material about the place we're heading for: Who has been there before? Did they find anything? Are the rocks of the right type and of the right age for us to find the kinds of animals we're looking for?

Once we've arrived at a site, our goal is to find fossils and get them home. First we walk around the site on reconnaissance, looking for small flecks of teeth or pieces of bone. After we've found some, we probe them gently with dental tools and small brushes, infusing the bones with very thin glue to harden them as we go. Working carefully, we try to

figure out exactly how much of the animal we've found and what animal it is.

At this point, when we have larger specimens, we mark them with a flag and take their coordinates. Using a global positioning system that employs satellites, we locate ourselves precisely so that we can find our way back. After several specimens have been located, we decide which one to excavate. This isn't easy. We have a small number of people to work on the specimen, only so much room in the truck, a short time to do the work in, and limited supplies. So this decision is crucial to the success of the expedition.

The decision is made on the basis of how important the specimen is, how difficult it will be to excavate it, and what kinds of animals we have to choose from. Obviously we would always like to excavate unique or very rare animals in rocks that are easy to dig in, but this isn't always possible.

After we've made the decision, we choose an excavation team. These are the people who will get the specimen out. The excavation team is not always the people who found the specimen or the people who did the original work on it. Often members of the crew have specific talents that we need for these kinds of jobs.

We begin the excavation by picking up all the loose and broken pieces of the skeleton and taking photographs to document where these fragments go and what the specimen looked like before we started working. Then we harden the bones by dumping lots of glue on the exposed pieces. Probing and brushing define the edges of the specimen before digging starts.

Digging is always the hard part. Fortunately, at Ukhaa Tolgod the rocks are generally very soft, so it's not as backbreaking as at other places where we've collected. But the work still generates plenty of sore muscles and blisters. The point of excavation is to carve out a sort of pedestal under the fossil, removing all the surrounding rock, then to dig in under it just a bit, so that it looks like a rock toadstool—a very valuable toadstool that may contain a spectacular specimen of a previously unknown dinosaur.

After the pedestal has been constructed, we cover it with wet newspaper (brought all the way from the United States) and strips of burlap or cheesecloth dipped in plaster of paris. This is called jacketing, and it's a very messy operation. We end up picking dry plaster off ourselves for days, and sometimes a fellow crew member even helps by throwing wet plaster on someone's back or in someone's hair.

After layers and layers of the plaster have been put on, our fossil is encased in a cast. Once the cast is dry, we break the top of the pedestal off its base and flip it over, hoping that what's inside will stay put. When the cast has been safely turned, we jacket the bottom using the same method.

Then all that's left is to get the specimen into a truck and get it back to camp. This sounds easy, but these specimens often weigh several hundred pounds and must be carefully lowered off the side of a cliff to get to the waiting truck. In camp before the end of the expedition, we put the specimen in a padded box for the long journey home across the desert and then the ocean. This process, although simple, works. In all the expeditions the museum has made to the Gobi, only a couple of specimens have arrived in New York damaged.

In many of the Late Cretaceous rocks in the Gobi Desert, specimens of *Protoceratops* are the most commonly found fossils.

During the 1923 expedition, the team had collected more than fifty dinosaur eggs. Three different kinds of eggs had been found, but most of them were a single type—about six inches long, shaped like an inflated hot-dog bun, with a surface covered by small ridges and bumps. Sometimes as many as thirteen eggs lay in a nest, distributed in a pattern like the spokes of a bicycle wheel. George Olsen's nest,

the first to be found and the one with the peculiar small dinosaur on top, was such a nest.

Because *Protoceratops* was the most common dinosaur found at the Flaming Cliffs, museum scientists thought that the most common kind of egg found at the site must belong to this small plant-eater. The announcement of the discovery of the eggs of *Protoceratops* was big news; it made Roy Chapman Andrews a celebrity, and the museum was packed with people wanting to see the discoveries. For seventy years the type of egg originally found by the 1923 expedition has been called the egg of *Protoceratops*.

But what about the small theropod? It got a bit lost in all the excitement surrounding the announcement of the egg find, but it wasn't totally ignored by scientists. It was a very weird animal, but at the time scientists concentrated more on its association with the *Protoceratops* nest than with its peculiar anatomy. What was it doing so close to that nest?

Henry Fairfield Osborn, the chairman of the museum's Department of Vertebrate

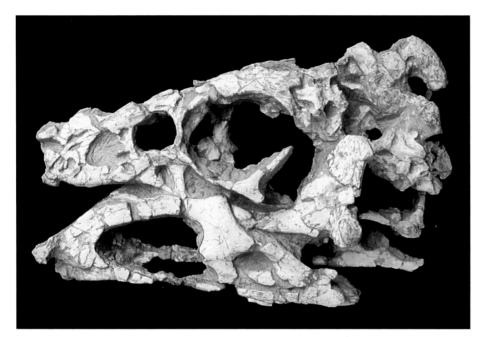

The first *Oviraptor* skull found is not well preserved. But when it was discovered, scientists recognized that it was similar in many ways to the skulls of birds.

story of the nasty *Oviraptor* chomping down on the defenseless *Protoceratops* nest has been told and written in scientific and popular books ever since.

What Was Oviraptor Like?

Paleontology, proposed that the animal had died during a fierce sandstorm while it was raiding the nest of the *Protoceratops*. Consequently, he named it *Oviraptor philoceratops* (*Oviraptor* for short). The name is based on a Latin translation of "egg stealer that is fond of *ceratops*" (short for *Protoceratops*). Osborn was cautious about using this name because he wasn't certain that the *Oviraptor* had really just been looking for a quick lunch. But the

Oviraptor was an unusual dinosaur. Compared to some of the more famous dinosaurs, like *Tyrannosaurus rex* and *Allosaurus,* it was rather small. An adult was only seven to ten feet long, which is about average size for theropod dinosaurs. *Oviraptor* was bipedal, which means it walked and ran exclusively on its two back legs. Its small skull was equipped with big eyes and a toothless beak. It had long forelimbs and a long neck.

Because *Oviraptor* is so unusual, figuring out even some pretty basic things, like what it ate, has been difficult. We do know a few things. For example, when it walked, it held its back parallel to the ground; its tail stuck straight out behind, counterbalancing its body. Like all theropods, *Oviraptor* had three

In life *Oviraptor* was a two-legged animal with big claws. It was probably an active, clever predator.

primary toes on each foot and a small fourth toe high up on the inside of the ankle. Each toe ended in a sharp claw. It also had long arms with three thin and elongated fingers on each hand. Each finger ended in a big hooked claw. In an adult *Oviraptor,* this claw was as long as six inches. *Oviraptor's* neck was long and, like a bird's, S-shaped.

The most unusual part of *Oviraptor* is the bizarre head. The skull is short and very high. The eyes are large, and the nose opening is small. The lower jaw has a strange shape, and it attaches to the rest of the skull by a sliding joint. This joint allows *Oviraptor's* jaw to slide front to back. Unlike most theropods, *Oviraptor* has no teeth. Instead there's a large parrot-like beak that in life was probably covered by a horny bill. On top of the head of some species of *Oviraptor* is a large crest, similar to the crests of some living birds like cassowaries and hornbills.

To us it seems reasonable that *Oviraptor* was a predator or scavenger. At least, the presence of large, sharp claws on the forelimbs points to this. Others have challenged this view, usually on the basis of the absence of teeth in *Oviraptor* and related animals. But as you know if you've ever watched an eagle or a hawk eat, a lack of teeth doesn't slow these creatures down.

Since the discovery of the original *Oviraptor* in 1923, several more specimens have been found. Most were collected by Russian-Mongolian and Polish-Mongolian expeditions. A few have been collected by Chinese-Canadian and Chinese expeditions in Inner Mongolia. Many of these specimens are more complete than the original *Oviraptor*. Some show variation in the form of the head crest. Perhaps these differences mean that there were external physical differences between males and females, or that differences developed

Oviraptor philoceratops

Ingenia

Oviraptor mongoliensis

Oviraptorids, like some groups of birds living today, displayed different and bizarre headgear. Perhaps this helped species recognize each other or marked differences between sexes.

with age. Or they could just be individual differences like the different shapes and sizes of moose antlers.

These various expeditions also found other kinds of *Oviraptor.* Together we call all these species oviraptorids. Two different species of smaller oviraptorids have been described in scientific papers. One is called *Conchoraptor* and the other *Ingenia.* Both come from Mongolia. Both are small—only about five feet long. *Ingenia* and *Conchoraptor* have body plans similar to that of *Oviraptor.* Both are bipedal, long-armed, three-fingered theropods. Like their larger cousin, they also lack teeth and have short skulls with large eyes. Unlike *Oviraptor,* they lack large crests on top of their skulls.

Oviraptorids at Ukhaa Tolgod

At Ukhaa Tolgod we've found a lot of oviraptorids. They're one of the most common dinosaur fossils we encounter. Not all of them are the same species, and the oviraptorid diversity at Ukhaa Tolgod is the greatest yet mea-

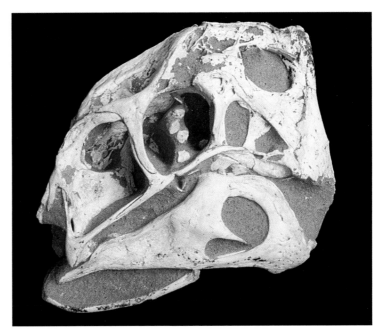

This well-preserved skull shows the structure of *Oviraptor's* crest.

sured. The most common type of oviraptorid fossil is a large form that's very similar to *Oviraptor* from the Flaming Cliffs. We've found several specimens of this animal, including one spectacular one.

This specimen preserves nearly every bone in the body. The head is one of the best theropod dinosaur skulls ever found, preserving every bone, even the small ones that support the lens of the eye, and the bones of the

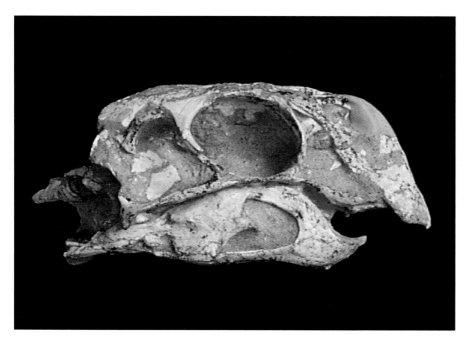

This skull may belong to an entirely new type of animal, or it could be the skull of an *Ingenia*.

middle ears. This is one of the largest oviraptorids known, almost twelve feet long. It was a crested form, although the crest is smaller and differently shaped than in some oviraptorids.

Two other kinds of oviraptorids from Ukhaa Tolgod are much smaller—only about five feet long. One has a skull that is short, very similar to that of *Oviraptor*, but lacks a large crest. Two specimens of this type were found lying just a foot or so apart. At first we wondered if these specimens might just be youngsters of the larger form with the crest.

However, when we had removed the first small oviraptorid specimen from the rock that entombed it, we could tell that it was not a young animal. This animal had reached its adult size and had stopped growing. What we had, then, was an adult of a species that had never been found before and didn't have a name.

The second type of small oviraptorid is different from the first in that the skull is long and low. It's also an adult, and it lacks a crest, but we won't know until we remove the skeleton from the rock whether it's a new kind of animal or an *Ingenia*. The skull of *Ingenia* has not been found; the fossils that have been discovered are only body parts. These body parts were different enough from *Oviraptor* for Mongolian paleontologists to justify giving it a new name, *Ingenia,* after a small town in Mongolia near where the specimen was found. Only after we compare the skeleton of our second small oviraptorid with the skeletons we have already identified will we be able to tell whether this is also an *Ingenia* or a new, unknown species.

Why were there so many oviraptorids at Ukhaa Tolgod? No one knows for sure, but it must have been a prime oviraptorid habitat. Just as some places in Africa today attract huge numbers of different but closely related antelope, something about Ukhaa Tolgod drew this collection of unusual animals.

Finding Eggs

There are many different types of eggs at Ukhaa Tolgod, and we find a lot of them. Some of the more common fossils are eggshell fragments. We find them at the base of almost every cliff; they're often very hard, so after they've been eroded out of the ground and are lying on the surface, they aren't destroyed as quickly as bones are.

The most common type of dinosaur egg from Ukhaa Tolgod is the familiar *Protoceratops*-type egg first found at the Flaming Cliffs by the Central Asiatic Expeditions. Since those trips this type of egg has been found in many other places throughout Asia. As we've said, these eggs are oblong and covered with small ridges and bumps. They're often found in clutches, or fossil nests that contain as many as twenty eggs. Usually the eggs are laid on their sides, in a circle that radiates out from a hollow space in the middle of the nest. Often there are two rows of eggs, and some nests even seem to show that the eggs were laid in pairs. Perhaps one egg was laid from each of the mother dinosaur's ovaries.

Looking at Eggs

We study eggs by examining their microstructure, looking at a small piece of an egg through a microscope—sometimes a powerful electron microscope. Under high magnification we can see the individual layers of the eggshell, and we can even observe the small pores that the developing dinosaur breathed through while it was inside the egg. Differences in these features can tell us interesting things about dinosaurs and give us hints about how dinosaurs are related to one another.

Scientists have looked at a lot of dinosaur eggs using this technique, and some important patterns have emerged. Many dinosaurs have a type of eggshell unknown in any living animal. Other eggshells that many scientists believe come from theropods resemble those of primitive living birds like the emu and ostrich. The *Protoceratops*-type eggs have this sort of microstructure.

Another clutch of eggs found at Ukhaa Tolgod has the same kind of microstructure as the *Protoceratops* type. It's shaped more like a chicken egg, has thinner walls, and has no bumps or ridges on its surface. Instead of being laid in a radiating pattern around a hollow space, the eggs are standing upright as if they were in an egg carton. There's no hollow area in the middle of the nest.

These kinds of eggshells had been found in other parts of the world, but no one knew what kind of dinosaur had laid them. But at Ukhaa we got lucky: Lying in the middle of this nest was a skeleton of a little dinosaur that had perished not long after hatching. We know that this skeleton is the remains of a troodontid, so the eggs must be troodontid eggs. Interestingly, these eggs have the same microstructure as the *Protoceratops*-type egg, and both types of eggs have the same microstructure as the eggs of birds.

The other dinosaur eggs at Ukhaa Tolgod don't contain embryos, so we can't tell which dinosaurs they belong to. But they're still interesting. They tell us that a great diversity of dinosaurs made Ukhaa Tolgod their home more than 70 million years ago. Some of the more exciting finds are a clutch of seventeen grapefruit-sized eggs with very thick shells. We have no idea what kind of dinosaur laid these because we have yet to excavate an animal big enough to have been the parent. Other eggs are tiny and may not be dinosaur eggs at all but could be the eggs of lizards or turtles. We can only hope to find more embryos that will help us figure out who laid what egg.

Three

Everything Changes

The day after our expedition first stopped at Ukhaa Tolgod in 1993, we made a discovery that changed the way we looked at dinosaurs. While prospecting an area of low-lying red hills, Mark Norell came upon a nest of dinosaur eggs. The eggs we found were oblong and had a wrinkled surface. In fact, they looked like the *Protoceratops*-type eggs found by Roy Chapman Andrews and his team seventy years earlier.

However, this discovery has to do with one egg, an egg laid in a nest 70 million years ago. This egg was grouped with several others in a radiating pattern around a hollow spot. Once the egg had been laid, development proceeded and the embryo transformed from a blob of dividing cells into something that looked like a baby dinosaur. Then, just before hatching, something happened. Maybe the nest was covered in a sandstorm when the parents were away, or maybe it was buried by slow-moving, muddy sand. Whatever happened, the developing egg was buried deeply enough that it lay untouched for millions of years.

On a hot July day in 1993, this egg was found broken open on the red ground of the fossil site at Ukhaa Tolgod that we called Xanadu. The tiny fossilized remains of the little embryonic dinosaur were exposed.

From ten feet away Mark could see the tiny white bones inside the broken egg. When he looked closer, the egg appeared too fragile to handle safely. We left it for a while so that we could go back to camp and get some glue to stabilize this important specimen. But Mark couldn't resist picking up part of the egg, the part that held the foot. From this single piece it was clear that this little dinosaur inside the *"Protoceratops"* egg was no *Protoceratops*. Instead of a foot with five toes, this little dinosaur showed a three-toed foot—just like theropods. This was definite proof that the eggs long considered to be the eggs of *Protoceratops* were really the eggs of a meat-eating dinosaur.

It was an exciting moment, but soon we got down to the job of collecting the specimen and packing it safely for the long journey from Ukhaa Tolgod back to New York. We knew we had an important find, but we still didn't know what kind of theropod dinosaur we'd found.

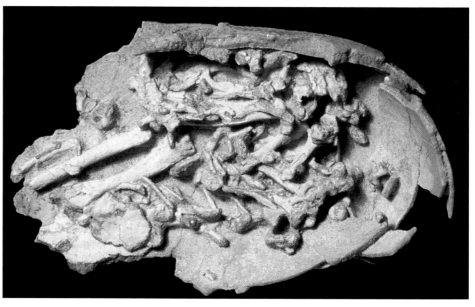

A couple of months later, back at the museum, we unpacked our treasure. Amy Davidson, a preparator and member of the expedition, immediately set to work on it. After only a couple of days, our field identification that this was the egg of a theropod and not a *Protoceratops* was confirmed. But it wasn't until a Mongolian colleague, Rinchen Barsbold, visited the museum that the identity became clear—our little dinosaur was an oviraptorid.

This specimen is the first theropod dinosaur embryo ever found. Its discovery cleared up the old misconception that *Oviraptor* stole other dinosaurs' eggs. Instead it suggested that *Oviraptor* was a good parent.

Under Amy's delicate hand, more of the dinosaur was exposed each day, until almost every grain of sand had been removed and we had our little dinosaur prepared on the half shell. Not all of the embryo was preserved. Much of the skeleton had been lost to erosion; if we had found the specimen a few years earlier, more of it would have been preserved.

Still, enough is there to visualize the little creature curled up in its egg, with its head tucked near its legs. The skull is mostly gone, but the nose, the floor of the braincase, and the bones that form the roof of the mouth are there, along with the lower jaw. The neck bones and most of the backbone segments and the hips are preserved. Only one of the

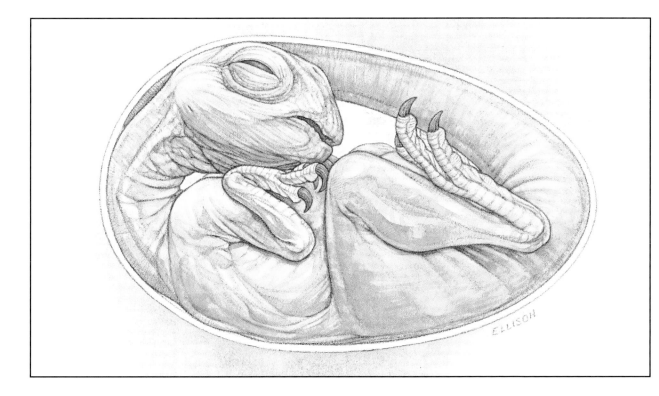

The embryo that was found at Ukhaa Tolgod had died just before hatching. This reconstruction shows the 80-million-year-old embryo just before it died and was fossilized.

27

arms and one of the legs are present, but both shoulder bones are there, as is the wishbone. The left leg is bent up toward the chin. The tail is missing.

This specimen completely changes *Oviraptor*'s bad reputation. *Oviraptor* was not a nasty dinosaur preying on the nest of a small plant-eater; it had died next to a nest of its own kind. The exact relationship of the adult to the nest was still unknown—that would require another great discovery, which we'll talk about later. Nevertheless, by drastically changing the way we look at this one dinosaur, this find illustrates an important point about science: With each new discovery, everything we believe is subject to change.

By studying the little dinosaur, we can learn a great deal about how it lived. One thing that's immediately obvious is that this little dinosaur died just before it was about to hatch. When animals with skeletons grow, it takes a long time for the skeleton to form. When some animals like crocodiles and birds hatch, much of their skeleton is made of soft cartilage that is not preserved as a fossil. As the animal matures, this cartilage is replaced by bone. This is most apparent on small bones and at the ends of big bones. In this case, however, even tiny bones like toe segments had been preserved. Because the skeleton was so well formed, we can tell that our embryo was about to hatch.

Some scientists believe that by looking at how well formed the bones of animals are when they hatch (how much is bone and how much is cartilage), they can tell something about juvenile habits. Today some birds, like ostriches and chickens, are very advanced when they hatch. These birds are called precocial birds. When they come out of the egg, they can already walk and feed. Their parents don't need to take care of them very long, and they don't spend much time in the nest after they hatch. Other birds, called altricial birds, like robins and eagles, have skeletons that are mostly cartilage. They depend on their parents for food and protection and spend a long time in the nest after hatching. Some critical regions, like the hips, are so weak that the young birds can't even walk for several days.

Compared to modern birds, our little oviraptorid had very well-developed bones. We think it's likely, based on this observation, that baby oviraptorids could walk and feed shortly after they hatched. They probably didn't spend too much time in the nest.

Since 1993 we've found several more embryos at Ukhaa Tolgod, but none of them appears as complete as the first one. Some of these are from different dinosaur species, although they're so poorly preserved that we can't tell exactly which species they belong to.

The Nester

Just a few days after we had discovered Ukhaa Tolgod, we located a fragmentary skeleton. At first all that was visible was a hand with three claws sticking out of the ground, along with thousands of small white flecks that were parts of the skeleton that had eroded from the hill. The claws immediately told us that the specimen was a theropod—probably an oviraptorid. They were big, so obviously this animal was an adult. But how

Spectacular fossils don't always look great when we find them. Here expedition members huddle around what became one of the most dramatic dinosaur specimens ever recovered—an oviraptorid preserved in a brooding position on its nest of eggs.

complete was the skeleton? Was it worth collecting? At first we didn't know, and we left it for a couple of days as we pursued more urgent projects.

After we had finished everything else, we came back to the weathered theropod skeleton and did some preliminary excavation. After a little work, it looked better than we'd thought. Besides the claws, the arm was there; then the

29

other arm revealed itself farther inside the hill. We still didn't know whether this specimen was good enough to use our meager remaining supplies of plaster and burlap on. Amy Davidson and Luis Chiappe, an expert in fossil birds, continued digging while the rest of the crew moved on to other projects.

Working at a site some way off, Mike Novacek and Mark saw Amy driving a jeep fast in their direction. Their first thought was that someone had gotten hurt. When she got close, however, Amy's smile gave it away—she had found something really good. She announced that the fragmentary skeleton was more complete than we'd thought. More importantly, it was sitting on top of a nest of eggs! This specimen was the second piece of the puzzle that both explained the original *Oviraptor* discovery and changed forever the way we look at dinosaurs.

It was obvious that the skeleton and the nest were associated. But as with all our specimens, we didn't uncover too much in the field—instead, we had to restrain our curiosity

Working in the field is dirty, dusty, and often uncomfortable, but when you make a spectacular discovery, none of that matters.

and wait to see what would be revealed in New York.

After the specimen had been safely jacketed, our next task was to get it into the truck—a Soviet military truck with a bed almost five feet off the ground. Our specimen weighed more than 400 pounds. In the rain we backed the truck as close as we could get it to the specimen. Then, with a Herculean effort, Americans and Mongolians all lifted together to hoist the heavy, wet block into the back of the truck. Safely loaded, with no injury among the crew except for a few skinned knuckles and strained muscles, the nester was ready for its trip north across the desert to Ulaanbaatar. There we would build a padded box for it and ship it by air freight via Beijing to New York.

Once we and the specimen were safely back in New York, after a period while museum technicians were busy on other projects, work finally began on the nesting dinosaur.

First Amy sawed off the plaster jacket around the specimen. Then she proceeded to clean the specimen with small air-powered

A skilled preparator works on the nester fossil brought back from our Gobi expeditions.

chisels, grinders, and needles. We'll never forget what happened over the next few weeks: A dinosaur sitting on a nest of eggs emerged.

What we were seeing was a snapshot of an event that happened more than 70 million years ago: A parent dinosaur died while sitting on its nest of eggs. A scientific paper was published on this specimen in 1995; a picture of the specimen appeared on the cover of the prestigious scientific journal *Nature*. It also appeared on the front page of nearly every major newspaper in the United States, and the story of the discovery was carried extensively on television and radio.

Not all of the specimen was preserved. Much had been lost to erosion, including the tail, head, and neck and most of the backbone. But what was left was remarkable. The arms were wrapped back around the perimeter of a nest that contained more than twenty eggs. The pelvis was right in the middle of the nest; the legs were tucked up underneath the body, just the way a brooding chicken sits. In fact, we could even make out the horny sheath that formed the outside of the claw.

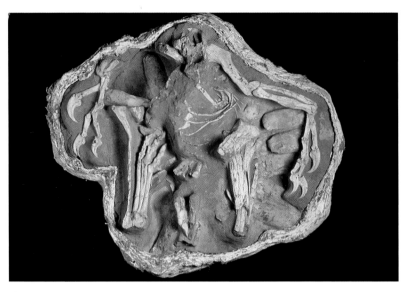

The oviraptorid is perched on its nest with its arm wrapped around its clutch of eggs.

What else do we know about this oviraptorid? Some things we can tell, others we can't. We can tell that the animal was an adult when it died. We can even tell that while it was alive the animal suffered an injury, a broken arm, which later healed. We can't tell whether it was a male or a female, though. The bones don't show us this, and among modern birds both males and females sit on their nests.

Does the fact that the nester was sitting on the nest mean it was warm-blooded? Modern birds are warm-blooded. They sit on their nests to transmit their body heat to the

What did this specimen tell us? First, it explained what the *Oviraptor* found in 1923 was doing so close to the so-called *Protoceratops* nest. That specimen had also died while sitting atop its eggs; unfortunately, it was not collected as carefully as ours, nor was it as complete, making such an interpretation at the time virtually impossible. The most important thing our specimen told us was that some dinosaurs brooded—that is, incubated their eggs by sitting on them, just as modern birds do.

The Ukhaa Tolgod oviraptorid may have looked like this, very similar to large modern birds such as ostriches.

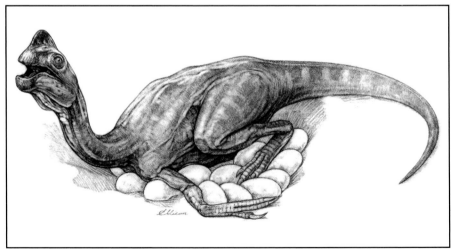

embryos inside the eggs. This process allows the embryos to develop. But we can't tell whether our nester was warm-blooded.

How did this animal come to die on the nest? That question has haunted us since we found the specimen. We'll probably never be able to reconstruct the events leading to the animal's death. Still, we can make a few inferences by looking at animals that brood today.

When birds sit on their nests for extended periods, they can't forage. They become weak and may lose up to thirty percent of their body weight. Maybe this is what happened to the Ukhaa Tolgod oviraptorid—it was weakened, or dead, and stayed on the nest while it was rapidly covered by sand or sandy mud. But we don't know.

Since the discovery of our nester in 1993, others have appeared. First, members of a Chinese-Canadian expedition released information about their new specimen. This specimen, although extremely fragmentary, can be interpreted in light of the Ukhaa Tolgod nester. It sits in the same posture above a fragmentary clutch of the same type of eggs.

Finding Other Animals at Ukhaa Tolgod

So far we've identified more than fifty kinds of fossil animals with backbones at Ukhaa Tolgod. They fall into four main groups: mammals, turtles, lizards, and dinosaurs.

The fossil mammals lived during the time of the dinosaurs, and although they looked like rats, hamsters, and shrews, they actually belong to several groups of very primitive mammals. Some are related

to mammals like us that have offspring by live birth. Others, like the deltatheridians, are related to modern pouched animals like opossums and kangaroos.

The commonest group of mammals we've found at Ukhaa Tolgod is the multi-tuberculates. These animals have no close living relatives. They resemble rodents, with paired chisel-like teeth, and probably had similar habits, gnawing on seeds, plants, and bugs.

Turtles at Ukhaa Tolgod are rare; only a couple have been discovered. But they're interesting because they help us understand the environment these animals lived in. Many turtles from the Late Cretaceous Period (about 72 million years ago, as we've said) have close living relatives, and it's pretty easy to tell the difference between turtles that live on land and those that make ponds or streams their home. At Ukhaa Tolgod we've found both types.

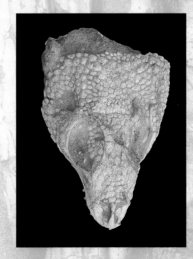

The lizard is the most diverse kind of animal we've found at Ukhaa Tolgod. We've discovered more than 500 specimens of 30 different kinds. Many of these are related to common animals today, like skinks and monitor lizards. One of the largest lizards, called **Estesia**, is closely related to the Gila monster. **Estesia** had grooves on its teeth just like the modern Gila monster. These grooves allow the Gila monster to transmit poison from its mouth to its prey. The presence of these grooves in **Estesia** suggests that this three-foot-long lizard was also poisonous and may have had similar habits and diet.

American Museum expeditions have even found another one of our own, this one during the 1995 season, in a fossil site at Ukhaa Tolgod called the Camel's Humps. This specimen, larger than the 1993 nester, is still fragmentary, although some parts, like the body and the tail, are better preserved. As of this writing, this specimen is still in its plaster field jacket awaiting preparation.

Dinosaurs Among Us

The discovery of the embryo and the nester are pieces in a puzzle that scientists have been trying to solve for a long time. Are dinosaurs extinct? The answer, we now know, is no. Dinosaurs are alive today, and you can see them in trees, in parks, and on your dinner table. Birds are living dinosaurs. Hard to believe? Let us explain.

Oviraptor and its close relatives, like *Conchoraptor* and *Ingenia,* are classified together in a group called Oviraptoridae. That group in turn belongs to a very advanced group of theropod dinosaurs called Maniraptora. The members of this group of dinosaurs have highly modified wrists, and many also have modified feet. Specifically the name Maniraptor refers to a small crescent-shaped bone in the wrist joint. This joint gives maniraptors extraordinary flexibility in their hands—a characteristic that would become very important in the evolution of the maniraptors. In fact, this evolutionary change directly links the maniraptors with their modern descendants, the birds.

What kinds of theropod dinosaurs are maniraptors? Not the giant ones like *Tyrannosaurus rex* or the really old ones like *Coelophysis* and *Eoraptor*. Most maniraptors are pretty small. Maniraptors have been divided into several subgroups. Besides the Oviraptoridae, the best-known ones include the Troodontidae, the Dromaeosauridae, and the Avialae.

Troodontids are very rare animals. Only a few good specimens have ever been found, all in Cretaceous Period rocks in Asia and North America. The oldest ones are found in the

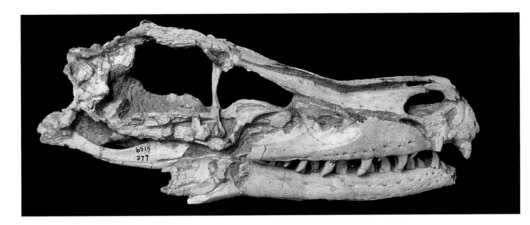

Dromaeosaurs came in different shapes and sizes. *Velociraptor*, left, was about the same size as a large fox or coyote and may have had similar habits.

Ordos Desert of northern China and are about 100 million years old. Several have been found in Mongolia. One of the first to be found was collected along with *Oviraptor* during the 1923 expedition to the Flaming Cliffs; it is called *Saurornithoides*. Another was collected by expeditions we participated in at Ukhaa Tolgod—one of us named it *Byron jaffei* after the son of a friend. The North American specimens all come from western North America. Troodontids had the largest brains in relation to their size of any theropod dinosaur except for birds.

The dromaeosaurs include familiar dinosaurs like *Velociraptor* (from Mongolia), as well as the fifteen-foot-long *Utahraptor*—the 110-million-year-old dromaeosaur found in the western United States. Dromaeosaurs even bigger than *Utahraptor* existed. They were found in Mongolia and are still awaiting study. Other familiar dromaeosaurs include the North American *Deinonychus* and *Dromaeosaurus*. At Ukhaa Tolgod we've found remains of a new, unnamed dromaeosaur that is closely related to *Velociraptor*. A few bones that may belong to dromaeosaurs have recently been found in North Africa.

Dromaeosaurs are astonishing animals. The dromaeosaurs' skeletons were lightly built. Their legs were long, and their tails were reinforced by stiffening rods. Presumably they were speedy. Dromaeosaur hands and feet sported large claws, including one highly modified giant claw on the second toe that has been called a killing claw. Dromaeosaurs' skulls were large, and they had serrated teeth.

The oldest avialian is an animal called *Archaeopteryx* from southern Germany. It lived about 13.5 million years ago. Only seven specimens have ever been found, the most

Archaeopteryx was the first link discovered between dinosaurs and birds, but only a handful of these fossils have been found. This, known as the Eichstätt specimen, is the best-preserved example.

recent one in 1997. *Archaeopteryx* didn't look that much like a bird except that it had feathers. In fact, its skeleton resembles that of a dromaeosaur. It had a long tail and teeth, and its wing (actually its arm) is identical to the arms of other maniraptors in that the bones of the wrist and hand are separate. In living birds these bones fuse into single elements. Nevertheless, the kinship of modern pigeons, ducks, quail, and eighteen thousand other kinds of birds with these early avialians is firmly established.

However, figuring out how these groups are related to one another and specifically which one of these dinosaur groups is most closely related to birds has not been easy. Birds are warm-blooded, take care of their young, fly, and have wishbones—that is, fused clavicles. Only birds have wishbones, and scientists believe that a wishbone is essential for flight. Now, oviraptorids, troodontids, and dromaeosaurs all have characteristics that make them candidates to be close relatives of birds. For instance, oviraptorids and dromaeosaurs both have wishbones and bony breastbones.

Many theropods besides birds had wishbones, like this *Velociraptor.* Wishbones are essential for flight in modern birds.

Troodontids don't. But troodontids share other features with birds that other maniraptors don't have.

The question of which of these dinosaur groups is most closely related to living dinosaurs—birds—is still unanswered. But new research has established that the dromaeosaurs are the closest relatives of birds. Avialians, especially primitive ones like *Archaeopteryx,* share many traits with dromaeosaurs. These include characteristics of the hips and the shoulders. Both birds and dromaeosaurs also have large spaces filled with air surrounding the brain. All this suggests that dromaeosaurs, like *Velociraptor,* are the group most closely related to birds.

Despite our uncertainty, we can still understand a lot about birds by looking at these dinosaurs. For instance, we already know that it isn't only birds that have a wishbone—because other dinosaurs like oviraptorids and dromaeosaurs do too. In a living bird, the wishbone helps the bird to fly, but because fossils show that it was present in nonflying relatives of birds, we know that the wishbone originated before birds evolved, for some other reason besides flight.

Our understanding of the history of birds and their parts is just beginning. New fossil finds are helping us to refine our theories. Discoveries of oviraptorids at Ukhaa Tolgod are key elements that will help us to unlock the secrets of how modern birds evolved.

Four

Is It All Worth It?

Birds today are the product of millions of years of evolutionary history, and the key to understanding this history is the dinosaurs. Think of it this way. Take a bird, any one you can think of. Have it and its relatives always been this way? Was it specially created with all the attributes we associate with birds today? Have birds always had feathers, taken care of their young, built nests, and left their white droppings on sidewalks and car windows?

The answer is no. All these characteristics and behaviors are the products of the evolutionary process, and many of them appeared long before birds existed. They evolved first in more primitive dinosaur or reptile groups. Studying those groups gives us insight into how birds got to be the way they are and to do the things they do.

Let's look at living animals. The closest living relative of the bird is the crocodile. Crocodiles and birds share a number of characteristics. They build nests and take care of their young. The young can even communicate with each other while they're still inside their eggs, using high-pitched squeaks. The parents also guard the nests. Our explanation for these similarities is that crocodiles and birds are descended from a common ancestor that also had these behavioral and physical characteristics.

Nonbird dinosaurs are also descended from this common ancestor, so we think it's likely that they also built and guarded nests and took care of their young. Beginning with the first fossil nests found by Roy Chapman Andrews and the American Museum's Central Asiatic Expeditions, we've retrieved evidence that to some extent supports this assumption. Dinosaur nests have been found all over the planet and across a broad spectrum of dinosaur species.

But what about those characteristics that aren't shared by crocodiles and birds—those strictly bird traits like having feathers, brooding, taking care of the young for long periods after hatching, and building a neat nest?

We have some fossils that show these things also, and oviraptorids are some of the best. For instance, from the nests of oviraptorids we've found, it's apparent that the eggs were manipulated into a circle. Modern birds manipulate their eggs in a similar way, but modern crocodiles don't. This means that while this behavior was present in the common ancestor of *Oviraptor* and birds, it evolved long after crocodiles split off from the ancestor of dinosaurs. Brooding behavior shows the same pattern.

Other fossils tell us about bird characteristics like parental care and the presence of feathers. For instance, the presence of youngsters larger than hatchlings in nests of the duck-billed dinosaur *Maiasaura* suggests that the baby dinosaurs stayed in the nest for extended periods after hatching. The only way animals like this could have enough to eat would be if the parents brought them food.

Other new specimens from China seem to suggest that small meat-eating dinosaurs that are not even as closely related to birds as *Oviraptor* is had a fluffy body covering. One interpretation of these specimens is that these are primitive varieties of feathers. This suggests that the common ancestor of birds and these Chinese dinosaurs had a fluffy body covering. If this suggestion is backed up by evidence, we'll suspect that *Oviraptor* had some kind of feathery covering, because it's descended from the same ancestor.

Finally, viewing modern birds as the product of millions of years of dinosaur evolution changes the way we perceive dinosaurs. Imagine that you could transport yourself back beyond 65 million years to the time of the nonbird dinosaurs. Some of the animals you would see would have a fluffy body covering and would perhaps be warm-blooded; they would have wishbones and build nests. Inside the nests the eggs would be carefully arranged, not scattered haphazardly. The parents would be on the nest, brooding, or stationed nearby to guard it. After the young had hatched, the babies would stay in the nest, growing on food left by the parents. In fact, there would be no difference between these animals, now long extinct, and the dinosaurs that today we call birds.

It may be hard to believe that the "egg-stealing" dinosaur that Roy Chapman Andrews and his crew first found more than seventy years ago has changed what we know about dinosaurs so completely, but it's true. *Oviraptor*, the embryo, and the nester are pieces in a 72-million-year-old puzzle that we're helping to solve. When we've finished,

we hope to have a complete picture that will show us how birds evolved.

So is it all worth it? In a word, yes. None of the problems we encounter can equal the excitement we feel when we're in the desert looking at a truly unique fossil find. Our work isn't always easy and it isn't always fun, but we are following our dream.

Glossary

armored dinosaurs dinosaurs such as ankylosaurs and stegosaurs whose bodies were protected by bony plates.

badland *or* **badlands** a geographic region marked by erosion, scarce vegetation, rugged ravines, and hills.

clavicle the collarbone.

Cretaceous Period the final part of the Mesozoic Era (see time scale, page 8).

deposit the layers of mud, sand, and pebbles that have accumulated in an area after being carried there by water and wind.

embryo an animal at any stage of development before birth or hatching.

excavation the process of removing a fossil from the ground by digging.

fossil any trace of an ancient organism; usually the remains or impression of an animal or plant that has turned to stone. Skin and soft tissues rarely become fossilized; bones and teeth more commonly do.

geology the study of rocks, minerals, and fossils and the processes that form them.

Jurassic Period the middle part of the Mesozoic Era (see time scale, page 8).

Mesozoic Era also called the Age of Dinosaurs; composed of three periods: the Triassic, Jurassic, and Cretaceous (see time scale, page 8).

microstructure the microscopic structure of the mineral crystals that make up a fossil.

ornithischians the group of dinosaurs composed of the "bird-hipped" plant-eaters; includes the two-footed dinosaurs, the armored dinosaurs, and the horned dinosaurs.

paleontologist a scientist who studies ancient life and its fossil remains.

prospecting looking for fossils exposed on the surface of the ground.

quarrying excavating fossils from a large pit in a fossil-rich layer of rock.

saurischians the group of dinosaurs composed of the "lizard-hipped" dinosaurs; includes all the meat-eaters and the largest of the plant-eaters (the sauropods).

stratigraphic section a drawing of rock layers in an area that describes their composition and thickness, as well as how they lie one on top of the other.

theropod a member of the order of Saurischia; a meat-eating dinosaur that walked on two legs.

Triassic Period the first part of the Mesozoic Era (see time scale, page 8).

wishbone a forked bone made up of two clavicles that are fused, or joined; found only in birds.

For Further Reading

Chiappe, L. M. "Dinosaur Embryos: Unscrambling the Past in Patagonia." *National Geographic,* December 1998.

Clark, J. "An Egg Thief Exonerated." *Natural History,* June 1995.

Currie, P. "The Great Dinosaur Egg Hunt." *National Geographic,* May 1996.

Dingus, L., and L. Chiappe. *The Tiniest Giants: Discovering Dinosaur Eggs.* Doubleday Books for Young Readers, June 1999.

Horner, J., and J. Gorman. *Maia: A Dinosaur Grows Up.* Museum of the Rockies, Bozeman, Montana, 1985.

About the Authors

MARK A. NORELL, Ph.D., is the chairman of the American Museum of Natural History's Department of Paleontology. He was coleader of many of the museum's Gobi Desert expeditions.

LOWELL DINGUS, Ph.D., directed the American Museum of Natural History's fossil hall renovation and served as head geologist on the museum's Gobi Desert expeditions, as well as many others.